Mine!

Written by
Sarah Hammond

Illustrated by
Laura Hughes

PaRragon

Bath • New York • Singapore • Hong Kong • Cologne • Delhi
Melbourne • Amsterdam • Johannesburg • Shenzhen

Kitty is in her bedroom.
Today, she is a café lady.

Kitty sets out her café things
– the pasta on the plates
and the biscuits in the bowls,
the cups on the saucers with the teapot
and the milk and the spoons.

Café is open!
Here come the customers!

Tea for Teddy in the tall cup.
Cakes for Pansy on the pink plate.
Biscuits for Bingo in the brown bowl.

kitty's Café

Knock, knock
on the café door.

Who could it be?

"Look, Kitty," says Mummy, **"Lea has come
to play and she's brought some chocolate cakes.
Can she be a café lady too?"**

"Let's take it in turns," says Kitty.
"You can be the helper first, Lea!"

"I know!" shouts Lea.
"Let's have some café music!
We can all dance."

"**Not like that!**" says Kitty. "And you're in **Teddy's** seat!"

"I know!" shouts Lea.
"Let's have a café competition!"
She makes a tower of biscuits
and balances them on her head.

"Look, Kitty! No hands!"
"Not like that!" says Kitty.
"Biscuits go in the **brown bowl!**"

"I know!" shouts Lea.
"The café needs some new customers!"
She fetches Rooster and Woolly Pony.

"Come on,
animals –
tea time!"

"Not like that!" says Kitty.
"The animals live on the **farm!**"

"My turn to be the café lady now!" sings Lea.

"No! This café is **MINE!"**
shouts Kitty and hides the teapot in her tent.

And the plates,

bowls,

spoons,

milk,

cakes,

the pasta, the biscuits,
the cups and the saucers and
Teddy and Pansy and Bingo.

"Café is closed!"

Inside the tent, it is dark.
Teddy is quiet.
Pansy goes to sleep. Bingo is still.
They don't want tea or cakes
or biscuits any more.

Knock, knock
on the tent door.
"It's raining out here,"
says Lea.
"Can we come in?"

Kitty cuddles Teddy up close. Now there
is room for Lea and the animals too.
Teddy smiles. Pansy wakes up.
Bingo is hungry again.

"I know!" shouts Kitty.
"Let's have an inside picnic!"

"Yesssss!!!"
says Lea.

Tea for Teddy in the tall cup.
Cake for Pansy on the pink plate.
Biscuits for Bingo in the brown bowl...

and chocolate cakes
for Lea and Kitty to share.

For Charlotte

S.H.

For Anthony

L.H.

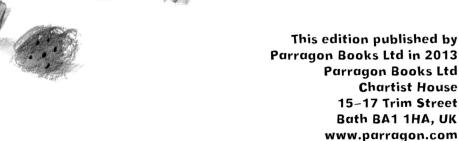

This edition published by
Parragon Books Ltd in 2013
Parragon Books Ltd
Chartist House
15–17 Trim Street
Bath BA1 1HA, UK
www.parragon.com

Published by arrangement with Meadowside Children's Books

Text © Sarah Hammond 2013
Illustrations © Laura Hughes 2013

ISBN 978-1-4723-1986-9

Printed in China